The MAGIC of NORUMBEGA

LENNA KUTNER

The MAGIC of NORUMBEGA

White Island Press

This book is a work of fiction. References to real people and locations are used solely to advance the fictional narrative. All other characters, and all incidents and dialogue, are drawn from the author's imagination and are not to be construed as real.

White Island Press
www.whiteislandpress.com

ISBN: 0692478442
ISBN 13: 978-0692478448

www.magicnorumbega.com

I am grateful to many people for their help with "The Magic of Norumbega."

Sandy Kirschenbaum scrutinized every word of the early manuscript, and frequently offered a better one. Later on, her technical assistance with formatting the book saved the day. Janet Linder, my fellow author, was always available with her editing suggestions and her calming advice. Susan Schale's creative eye guided my decisions about the cover illustration, and I'm so happy with the end result.

I would also like to thank my "junior editors" for their valuable insights and suggestions. From Auburndale, MA: Emma Brignall, Ilan Friedman, Jonas Helman, Natalie Martin, Alex Morefield, Poppy Needham, Julian Phillips, Christina Schmidt-Hong, Ella Sian, Max Sian, and Kate O'Leary's 2014-15 third grade class at the Williams School. From the Renaissance Montessori School in Fort Myers, FL: Grace Basey, Koan DiPiero, Joshua Duarte, Charles Dupre, Grace Hilliker, Katelyn Kelley, John Kehayas, Ellis Oliver, and Caden Stalter.

I had the pleasure of speaking with many people who enjoyed reminiscing about Norumbega Park. Chip Hayward was especially generous with his stories and memorabilia.

The photos at the end of the book of Norumbega's bygone days are from a collection maintained by Historic Newton. I'd like to thank Historic Newton as well as Joe Hunter from Remember Productions for providing them.

Most of all, I'm so grateful to, and for, my family: my husband Bob, whose enthusiasm for this book has been a wonderful gift, and my son Danny, for whom I wrote the story many years ago when he was "Geti's boy."

Contents

Chapter One

Music in Dog Park

EVERY DAY, dogs from all over town gathered in Dog Park to play. They spent their time running and swimming, chasing each other, barking at geese, wrestling, and rolling in the smelliest mud they could find.

All except Geti; she preferred to dance.

"Can't you hear the music?" she asked the other dogs. "Can't any of you hear it?"

The dogs shook their heads, or shrugged, or snickered and rolled their eyes. "All we hear are ordinary park sounds," her friend Murphy informed her for at least the one-hundredth time. "There isn't any music here. You don't see anyone else dancing, do you?" she added.

Geti knew the other dogs were wrong; there was music in Dog Park. Sometimes she barely noticed it, but other times it followed her from one end of the park to the other. She heard songs in the breezes that whistled through the tree branches. She felt rhythms pulsing over the field where she chomped on dandelion patches. Harmonies drifted in the river, and Geti tried to imagine the instruments that could have produced those sounds. She would cock her head and lift her ears, and listen as hard as she could to far-away bits of melody swirling through the air.

She could hear the music everywhere in Dog Park, but no matter how much she searched, she couldn't find its source anywhere. It was everywhere and no-where, and no one else could hear it. What was she supposed to think? It was obvious to her that this music was magical.

One morning Geti came across Murphy foraging in the field for a stick to chew. They kept each other company for a while until Murphy said, "Could you please stop twirling? You're making me dizzy."

"But I'm dancing to the music!" Geti explained in a

sing-song voice, swiping Murphy's face with her bushy red tail as she spun.

Murphy snorted. "I'm getting a little tired of hearing you talk about 'the music.' It makes you sound so strange. Magical music? Or is it musical magic? I can't keep it straight."

Geti thought it shouldn't be so hard to keep a small but important detail like that straight. "Well, I'm not crazy, and I'm not making it up," she declared firmly.

Instead of arguing, Murphy bounced against Geti and knocked her down. Tufts of Geti's long copper-colored fur and Murphy's short mustard-colored fur flew through the air as the large dogs rolled together playfully in the grass.

When they stopped to take a breath, Murphy stood up and said, "I love you, Geti. You're my best friend. I just wish you'd daydream less and play with me more."

"I love you right back," Geti answered. "But I wish you believed in the magic."

Murphy turned away, shaking her head in bewilderment, and ran off to the other side of the field. Barely noticing that she had left, Geti continued to twirl.

She danced until the music faded away. Then she remembered to look for Murphy, and spotted her standing alone, listlessly sniffing a bush. She bounded over to her friend and asked, "Are you mad at me?"

Murphy grunted without looking up.

"I'm sorry!" Geti said. "I know you just wanted to play with me." She sprang into action, hoping to make things right between them. She found a thick, sturdy stick and waved it in front of Murphy's nose, saying, "This is for you. It'll be perfect for chewing!"

Murphy accepted the stick from Geti, but instead of gnawing on it, she shouted, "Tug-of-war!"

The two friends raced down the hill to the river, their long legs nimbly leaping over tree roots and rocks, wrestling the stick between them. Just as they approached the riverbank, Geti again noticed the faint sound of music rippling over the water. Her ears began to flutter, and a swarm of shivers traveled from her nose to her feet. She couldn't stop herself from dropping her end of the stick. "Do you hear that?" she asked breathlessly.

"Nope!" was Murphy's muffled reply, her mouth still clamped onto the other end of the stick. She used it to nudge Geti lightly in the shoulder. "We're in the middle of a game, remember?"

"Listen, Murphy!" Geti insisted. "If you listen harder, maybe you can hear it this time."

As soon as Geti finished speaking, she could see that Murphy had finally run out of patience; her friend's tail stiffened, and her ears folded back as she tossed the stick away. Geti braced herself for Murphy's sharp reply, but before another word could be uttered, a croaky voice interrupted.

"I can hear it! I never knew dogs can hear the music, but frogs can. Well, not all frogs can hear it. But I can!"

Geti and Murphy stared with surprise at a small frog sitting on a lily pad. Dogs and frogs are not particularly fond of each other, and don't converse very often.

"It sounds like this, right?" the frog asked. He opened his mouth wide while his throat bulged like a small balloon.

And this is the sound that came out of him:

♪ croak ♫croak ♫croak♪ ♪ccccrroakkk♫

"Is he singing?" Geti whispered to Murphy.

"Make him stop, please!" Murphy whined, her nose wrinkling and her tail drooping between her legs. The frog grimaced back at her and croaked even louder.

"Frog! Hey, Frog, where is that music coming from?" Geti shouted over the noise he was making.

The frog stopped singing. "From Norumbega," he answered matter-of-factly.

"Where's Norumbega?" asked Geti at the same time Murphy asked, "What's a Morungeba?"

"Well, why should I tell you? I won't tell you!" he said, acting like a typical frog. But when he saw the disappointed look on Geti's face, his attitude softened.

"I suppose I could tell you how to find out for yourself," the ornery creature finally said, "but don't come crying to me when things go badly."

He sighed deeply, but continued. "There are magic words that will take you to Norumbega. Repeat the same words when you're ready to come back, and the rhyme will bring you home."

Geti was fascinated and her attention was focused on everything the frog was saying, but Murphy seemed simply annoyed by his foolishness. "Why waste your time with a frog?" she whispered in Geti's ear.

"Just remember," the frog sternly warned, ignoring Murphy. "Don't let Cushman catch you! The magic only works if you're free to leave. If he captures you, you'll belong to him and the words will be useless."

"Who's Cushman?" Geti asked, completely confused.

"Find out for yourself," the frog snapped.

He hesitated, and Geti was sure he had changed his mind again. "Please," she pleaded, while Murphy lay down and indifferently began cleaning her paws with her coarse tongue. "I just need to know!" Geti said, hoping the frog would understand.

"Relax! I'm getting around to it. The first thing you'll need to do is close your eyes and concentrate hard," the frog said. "Now listen carefully, because I'm only going to say the words once." Then he tightly squeezed his eyelids together and slowly began reciting a poem in his low, raspy voice:

"To Norumbega
In times long past
Where memories made
Will forever last.
Then home again
Where I belong
But in my heart
Norumbega's song."

And when the last word was croaked, the frog disappeared.

Chapter Two

Follow the Frog

GETI'S MOUTH dropped open as she stared at the empty lily pad. "Whoa," she finally managed to say, her voice full of awe.

Murphy stared at it for a moment as well. She jumped to her feet as the fur on her back puffed up in apprehension. Then she shook herself hard to settle her hackles back down, and gave her tail a firm swish.

"It was a trick," she declared scornfully. "He probably dove under the lily pad."

"But he could hear the music," Geti reminded her. "He knew those magic words!"

"Geti, anything that a silly frog knows is not something worth knowing. Let's go back up the hill now. I'm tired of this game."

The distant music had dissolved into thin wisps that no longer held a tune, and Murphy was galloping back up to the field. Geti took one last look at the lily pad. It was still empty and the frog was nowhere in sight. *I'm certain it wasn't a trick*, she thought. She trudged up the path behind her friend, wishing she could have somehow followed the frog instead.

The dogs zigzagged around tree trunks with a group of their friends who were playing tag, but Geti felt distracted. She couldn't stop puzzling over the whereabouts of the frog and the meaning of his words. When a misty rain began to fall, she left the game and wandered over to her favorite spot for daydreaming, in the shadow of a towering copper beech tree. Its sprawling branches arched so low they almost reached the ground. Geti snuggled in a bed of buttercups, nearly hidden beneath the tree's leafy limbs.

She closed her eyes and pondered each word of the magic rhyme. The name 'Norumbega' echoed over and over in her mind. The rain grew heavier and drummed on the leaves above her head, lulling her. Dog Park slowly melted away.

Suddenly Geti found herself in the river. "How did I

get here?" she wondered, and then got caught in a swift current that wouldn't let her go. As it swept her away from her beloved park, hordes of pint-sized green frogs encircled her and sang in a thundering chorus, "Cushman! Cushman! Cushman!" while Murphy shouted, "Don't come crying to me!"

Geti woke from her nightmare with a gasp. The shower had stopped while she slept and the sun was shining again. Under its gaze, the raindrops clinging to the grass sparkled like rhinestones. Suddenly everything in the park felt enchanted. It felt like anything, anything at all, could happen.

Geti stood up and pushed the bad dream from her mind. She looked around for Murphy but didn't see any of the dogs; she could only hear their frisky barks and

yelps in the distance. She told herself there would be no harm in a quick trip to see Norumbega. She was certain that she would return to Dog Park before Murphy had a chance to notice she was gone.

Geti's legs were trembling so she steadied herself against the tree's mighty trunk. Then she closed her eyes tightly as the frog had done, took a deep breath, and recited the words she hoped would answer all her questions:

"To Norumbega
In times long past
Where memories made
Will forever last.
Then home again
Where I belong
But in my heart
Norumbega's song."

For a moment, nothing seemed to happen. There was deep silence; even the birds had stopped chirping. Then all at once, in an explosion of sound, Geti was surrounded by human voices and laughter.

Her eyes sprang open and she looked around in amazement. The field overgrown with weeds and wild-flowers was gone, replaced by a neat lawn and paths dotted with benches. Families strolled hand in hand in all directions, chatting and licking drippy ice cream cones. To her left, where just yesterday she had chased a chipmunk into the woods, a Ferris wheel carried delighted children high up into the clouds and slowly back down again. The aroma of sausages and cotton candy made her mouth water.

When a large twig fell from overhead and landed at her feet, Geti noticed that even the copper beech tree was different. Its trunk seemed slimmer, and she was no longer shrouded by its branches. They were shorter than they had been just a moment ago.

"Could this be Norumbega?" she wondered aloud, her excitement rising.

"It is! This is Norumbega!" a bellowing voice above her head exclaimed.

Geti eagerly looked up into the highest branches of the tree, and then froze with terror as she tried to make sense of what she saw. A huge animal was perched above her head. Bristly fur covered him from head to toe, and his powerful legs hugged the branch, which bowed under his heavy weight. One of his massive paws was raised, its long claws gleaming in the sunlight.

"I was starting to think that you'd never look up," the black bear roared. "Welcome! Welcome to Norumbega Park!"

Chapter Three

Dune in the Tree

THE SIGHT of a bear sitting in the copper beech tree took Geti's breath away. Her ears flattened against the sides of her head, and her lips curled up to bare her teeth. She tried not to think about how puny they were compared to the fangs in the bear's mouth, and she knew her fierceness would be more convincing if she could stop her entire body from shaking.

Then the bear said, "Do you like ice cream?"

"Huh?" was the only response Geti could manage.

The bear made a sound that could have been a

growl, but sounded more like a laugh. In a softer voice, he said, "Did I startle you? I'm sorry. Let's begin again. My name is Dune. What's yours?"

"G… G… G… Geti," she squealed in a shaky voice that sounded nothing like her own.

"G-G-G-Geti?" the bear echoed, and made the gruff sound again. This time she was certain it was a laugh.

Geti swallowed hard and she willed her body to stop trembling. *This is another thing Murphy will never believe!* she thought, and fought back her own impulse to giggle.

"My name is Geti," she told the peculiar bear with more confidence in her voice. His playfulness made her fear seem silly, and she let it slip away. "Is this really Norumbega?" she asked.

"What else could it be?" said the bear.

"Well, I'm a little confused," she admitted. "A moment ago I was in Dog Park, and now I'm here."

"Oh, I see," Dune said, nodding his huge head. "That could be confusing!"

Geti tried to be patient while she waited for more information, but the bear seemed to have already forgotten about her. He was staring off into the distance, shading his eyes with his paw as though he was searching for something. "Yes?" she prodded him.

Dune turned his attention back to her, chuckling. "I've met birds and frogs from Dog Park over the years, and a squirrel once. But now that I think about it, I've never met a dog from Dog Park!"

When he saw the quizzical look on Geti's face, he tried to explain things more clearly. "You haven't really left your park at all, G-G-G-Geti. You've just traveled backward in time. You're visiting the past. This is what Dog Park was like a long time ago, long before you were born. It was a park meant for people."

"Oooh!" Geti exclaimed, her imagination popping as she listened to Dune.

She looked around in wonder, watching thoughtfully as some parents helped their children climb aboard a miniature train for a ride around a track. There were a lot of happy hoots and chatter; no one seemed concerned that a bear was sitting in the tree. That struck Geti as very odd, and she worked up the nerve to ask Dune about it.

"Dune, what is a bear doing in a people park?"

The branch beneath Dune creaked and swayed as the bear bobbed with laughter. When he finally settled down, he took his time answering Geti's question.

"I live in the Norumbega Zoo, over by the river, and I escaped while everyone was asleep," he explained. "I climbed up the tree before any of the visitors arrived. No one bothers to look up, so they don't even realize I'm here!"

"How did you manage to escape?" Geti asked, amazed by Dune's story.

"I just jiggled the lock on my cage until the door opened. I've done it lots of times," the bear announced proudly. "There's not a lock in the world that can hold me."

"If I lived in a zoo, I'd escape too!" Geti exclaimed.

"Oh, I don't mind the zoo," Dune corrected her. "I just love ice cream. When the animal trainer notices I'm gone, he'll know exactly where to find me. And he'll bring me a bucket of ice cream to coax me back to my cage. That's why I escape, for the ice cream! I'll share some with you if you'd like. You'll see. He'll be here in a little while."

This was all so different from the life Geti knew. She was silent for a moment, trying to sort it all out, when Dune interrupted her thoughts. "See, I told you!" he said in an excited voice, looking off into the distance again. "Here comes Cushman with my ice cream."

A feeling of panic swept over Geti. She had only been in Norumbega for a few minutes, and she was already crossing paths with Cushman. What had she gotten herself into? Her head filled with the croaky chant from her nightmare: "Cushman! Cushman! Cushman!"

"Oh no!" she cried. "The frog warned me to stay away from Cushman. Where can I hide?"

"Hmmm." Dune thought for a moment while Geti sprinted around and around the tree, unable to decide on which direction she should run. He surveyed the park from the vantage point of his branch.

Finally the bear said, "I know! You can hide on the merry-go-round. The giraffe has been sent off for repairs, so you can take his place. But... what about the ice cream?"

"Good-bye. Maybe I'll see you again sometime," Geti called as she ran off in the direction Dune pointed. She didn't stop to answer his question.

"Goodbye, G-G-G-Geti!" Dune shouted, just as Cushman reached the tree. They both watched with interest as Geti scampered away.

Chapter Four

The Carousel

G ETI RAN as fast as she could in the direction of the Ferris wheel, and just beyond it she spotted the merry-go-round. Ordinarily she would have stopped to admire the magnificent animals on the carousel. They were large and colorful, and looked so real it was hard to believe they were carved from wood. But there was no time for that now.

Just as Dune had promised, there was an empty spot between the tiger and the elephant. The merry-go-round slowed to a stop to let some children off, and other children rushed to climb aboard. In the hustle and bustle, Geti was able to slip through the crowd un-noticed.

She hopped onto the platform and tried to catch her breath. Holding her head high, she stood as majestically as she could in place of the giraffe. The colors in her long coat glistened in the sun, and Geti looked as though she were a statue handsomely painted in red and gold and orange.

The children were choosing their animals with great care. "Which lovely animal do you want to ride?" Geti heard one mother ask.

To her dismay, a little voice shouted, "I want to go on the doggy!"

"The dog is the only animal without reins to hold. Why don't you go on the ostrich instead, Danny?"

"I WANT TO RIDE ON THE DOGGY!" little Danny insisted.

"Well, okay," his mother relented. "Hold on very tightly to the dog's ears, so you don't fall off."

Geti tried to remain perfectly still while the child climbed onto her back. "Giddyap," he yelled as he poked the heels of his shoes into her sides. Music flowed from an organ in the center of the platform, and the merry-go-round began to glide. Geti wasn't sure which was worse, the boy bouncing on her back and tweaking her ears, or the topsy-turvy feeling that

swished in her stomach as the carousel carried her round and round and round.

"Burrrrp!" A big belch escaped from Geti's lips, and the child immediately cried, "This dog is alive, Mommy. It's really alive." Danny's mother smiled and waved, the boy thumped up and down on Geti's back with excitement, and Geti blurted, "Burrrrp! Ouch! Burrrrp!"

Once her queasiness settled down, Geti tried to keep her body tense and motionless, only allowing her eyes to dart about. She caught sight of Dune and Cushman for a few seconds each time the carousel completed a full circle. The jolly bear was walking on his hind legs, happily slurping ice cream from a huge container he carried with his front paws. Cushman gently led him with a leash. The park visitors stepped aside to give them room to walk, but applauded and laughed, seeming to believe that this was a show for their entertainment. Cushman had a broad grin on his face, and occasionally took a deep bow.

Cushman was a big fellow wearing red suspenders over a shabby white undershirt. The suspenders held up dark blue pants, which rested just below his heavy belly and hung an inch above his mud-covered shoes. His grey hair was combed straight back from his forehead, and he had a long mustache drooping around his lips. He wore glasses over his steel-blue eyes.

Geti didn't think the man looked very threatening at all. *Could the frog have been wrong about Cushman?* she wondered. Dune didn't seem afraid of him. *But I'd never want to be caged in a zoo, no matter how much ice cream I was offered!*

Geti's body ached. With Cushman out of sight, she rearranged her position to get a bit more comfortable. The child on her back screeched again. Just when Geti decided she couldn't stand the carousel for one moment longer, it glided to a stop. Children jumped off and children climbed on, and when everyone was settled, Geti was gone.

Chapter Five

The Ringmaster

AFTER GETI jumped off the carousel, she set out to explore Norumbega. Now and then she passed a tree or a bush that seemed like a young version of an old friend, but the other sights and smells of Norumbega were nothing like Dog Park.

Walking paths sprawled in every direction, each leading to entertainment and food. A clown wobbled past her, juggling bowling pins while walking on stilts. He was followed by a jester pedaling a unicycle and squawking out a tune on a kazoo. Geti briefly joined a group of people gathered around some acrobats who were displaying their skill at somersaults and backflips, twisting their bodies so quickly they blurred before her eyes. She watched them until she made friends with a little girl who shared bits of fried dough whenever her mother glanced away.

More walkways led to more wonders. Mechanical rides that looked like cars and seaplanes ferried children around the park. Women in uniforms played softball in an open field, surrounded by fans that cheered each swing of the bat. Other people tried their luck by hurling darts at balloons to win prizes.

Geti sprinted from one attraction to the next. She began plotting how to convince Murphy to come along on her next visit, imagining the fun they would have exploring the park together.

Late in the afternoon, Geti noticed a tall fence with an open gate. She peeked inside and saw a small crowd of people seated on bleachers around a circular stage where a man and six white horses were performing. Geti wandered in to see the show.

The horses wore tiaras of wilted feathers on their heads, frayed ribbons braided into their tails, and bells on red leather straps around their ankles. The man was dressed like a ringmaster, wearing a tall black hat and a black coat that was short in the front and longer in the back. He held a whip in his hand, which he waved about as he shouted commands to the horses: "Kneel! Curtsy! Dance!" Every once in a while he cracked the whip into the air. It made a quick, loud noise like a firecracker, and the horses responded by prancing a little higher and holding their heads a little taller. But after a few minutes, they would slow down again, their heads drooping as though holding them up was too much of an effort. The horses seem very old, or tired, or sad.

Geti watched from the entrance. The audience, she noticed, was not impressed with the show on the stage. There was a great deal of chatter and not much applause; a few people got up from their seats and left. Geti decided to leave, too. The show gave her an unsettled feeling, and she wondered if Norumbega was not as perfect as it had first seemed.

As she turned to leave, Geti felt a cold shiver go through her body. She glanced over her shoulder at the man on the stage, and found his icy blue eyes staring right at her. She hadn't recognized Cushman at first because his eye glasses were gone, and his droopy mustache had been combed into two curls plastered against his cheeks. When he saw her looking at him, he threw his head back and laughed. It was the nastiest sound she had ever heard.

Geti turned quickly and started to run, but to her horror, Cushman abandoned the horses to take chase.

He leaped off the stage and followed right behind her through the open gate. People in their path jumped out of the way to make room for the pair. Someone shouted, "Go Dog!" and they all took up the cheer.

"GO DOG!" "GO DOG!" "GO DOG!"

Geti was a fast runner but Cushman, despite his large size, kept her within his sight. "To Norumbega in times long past," Geti tried to say out loud as she ran, but the magic words came out as ragged, incomprehensible growls, and only slowed her down. She gave up and concentrated on increasing her strides instead.

Cushman chased Geti past a picnic area, past a ride where children swayed from side to side in giant spinning teacups, past the entrance to the zoo. Somehow he managed to stay on her trail, but when she saw the river ahead of her, Geti knew how she would escape.

She ran frantically along the water's edge, looking for a place to dive in and swim. There was none to be found. Children splashed and played games all along the shoreline, while hundreds of brightly colored boats glided between Norumbega and the opposite shore. Geti was sure to be hit with an oar if she tried to swim between the boats. But she was wasting precious moments. She could almost feel the ground shudder from the **THUD! THUD! THUD!** of Cushman's heavy footsteps. She had to get across that river.

There was a boat ramp alongside the swimming area. Geti jumped on and ran to the end of it. She crouched, aimed, and dove through the air.

She landed right on target, on the seat of a wooden canoe between two young women who were too startled to say a word. The canoe wobbled to the left, then teetered to the right. As soon as it was steady, Geti was off again. This time she landed on a boat built to look like a swan, filled with children who squealed with glee at the unexpected visit from the big red dog. From there, Geti sprung onto a bright blue paddle boat, then onto a yellow one, then on to another canoe, and so on, until she had crossed the entire river and was safe on the other side.

When she reached the shore, Geti turned around to look back at Cushman. He, too, had decided to cross the river by jumping from boat to boat, but he wasn't as graceful as Geti. As the dog was reaching safety, Cushman was being pulled out of the river by two lifeguards. He was sputtering mouthfuls of angry threats as water streamed from his sleeves and his tall hat bobbed downstream. All the way across the river, Geti could hear Cushman thunder, "I'm going to get that dog, no matter what I have to do!" He shook his fist and vowed to everyone who was gawking and laughing at him: "I'll show you! Come see Cushman's Animal Act! That dog is going to be the new star of my show!"

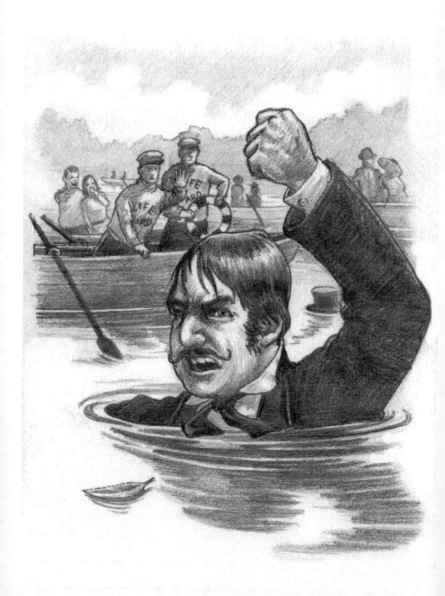

Chapter Six

Across the River

GETI SAT across the river from Norumbega and tried to calm down. She longed for the safety and peace of Dog Park. There was nothing more in Norumbega that she had any interest in seeing. All she could think of now was getting as far away from Cushman as possible.

She stood up, shut her eyes, and said the words that would take her home:

> "To Norumbega
> In times long past

Where memories made
Will forever last.
Then home again…

♪♫ bbbRRRuuummmppp ♪♫

Geti abruptly stopped speaking as the air filled with music. It wasn't the organ music that she had heard at the merry-go-round, and it wasn't anything like the scratchy jingles playing at the game arcades and food concessions throughout the park. This music was full and rich and it made her skin tingle. This was the music she used to hear softly in Dog Park, but now it was powerful and lively, and it almost swept her off her feet. It was the most enchanting sound she had ever heard. This was the music of Norumbega; this was the reason Geti had come in the first place. How had she forgotten?

Geti's tail began to wag and her feet began to tap. Her body swayed from side to side. Before she could stop herself, Geti was dancing.

"I can't go home yet," she cried, pushing thoughts of Cushman out of her mind. "I have to go back to Norumbega and find that music!"

It was almost dusk and Geti knew her best chance of getting across the river without being seen was to wait until dark. She hoped the boaters would go home when the sun set, but they did not. It was a hot night and boats continued to drift lazily on the water. When the people draped canopies of netting over their canoes to keep out the mosquitoes, Geti began to realize they were going to stay on the river late into the night, as long as the music continued to play.

Without warning, the darkened sky over the river was lit by a bright spotlight. Everyone looked up to see what was happening. Geti looked up, too. She heard an announcement coming from the Norumbega shore.

"Ladies and Gentlemen! Please direct your attention one hundred feet above the river! Norumbega is proud to present: *The Amazing Mazie*, our star iron-jaw acrobat. Watch her as she crosses the river by rolling along a high wire, holding on with only her teeth!"

The beam of light illuminated two tall, thin towers. Geti could see that one was positioned at the edge of the river in Norumbega. The second tower, slightly shorter, was directly across the river, just a few yards from where she stood. A sloped wire ran between the towers, high above the water. A mouthpiece, which resembled a horse's bit, was fastened to the wire with a ring, and a woman in a star-spangled tutu clung to the mouthpiece with her teeth. The spotlight followed Mazie as she slowly glided along the wire, dangling dangerously over the river. The audience below craned their necks to look upwards, watching breathlessly.

While the onlookers "oohed and aahed" and applauded Mazie as she traveled east to west above the river, Geti quickly and quietly swam west to east in the darkened waters below. She hoisted herself back onto the shores of Norumbega just as the trapeze artist was taking her bows.

Chapter Seven

The Ballroom

ONCE SHE was back on the grounds of Norumbega, Geti had no trouble following the sounds of the music. She pranced and hopped and skipped to the beat of the delightful tunes. They led to a building with large arched windows on all sides. The music poured out of each open window.

She knew it was risky, but Geti just had to see inside. She was certain her daydreams were about to come true. She found a spot in the back of the building where a window was unlit and hidden by a clump of bushes. Balancing on her rear legs while her front paws

caught onto the window ledge, Geti stretched her neck for a view of the room.

"Oooh!" she gasped with pleasure. Here it was: the magic she had longed to find.

The room was vast and elegant. At one end, at least thirty musicians stood on a stage playing their instruments more joyously than Geti could ever have imagined. The ballroom was bursting with the blare of trumpets, the wail of saxophones, the vibration of drums, the bellow of trombones, the velvety peal of French horns, the crash of cymbals. It all came together in a jubilant blend of sounds. A few people, dressed in their fanciest clothes, snuggled on small plush couches and listened to the music. Hundreds more flew around an enormous wooden dance floor, the men twirling their dance partners or swinging them high into the air. Chandeliers hanging from the ceiling sprinkled colored lights onto the dance floor, first blue, then green, then red.

The brilliance of the music was spellbinding, and Geti could feel it take hold of her. She jumped down from the window and she, too, began to dance.

For most of the night Geti danced beneath the window of the ballroom. The music seemed to lift her off the ground like an autumn leaf caught in a breeze. She spun and leaped and pirouetted, and felt happier than she had ever felt before. She danced until all the people went home, until all the musicians packed away their instruments and shut off the lights. Even then she danced some more, with the music playing in her head, until her tired legs began to feel like sponges that could barely hold her up. Finally, exhausted, she lay down on the soft grass. Before she could even begin thinking about what a magical day it had been, Geti was asleep.

Almost nothing could have woken her, not even the heavy footsteps circling her slumbering body.

Geti was still in a deep sleep, dreaming about dancing bears, when somebody started pulling at her, attaching something to her neck. "No, I don't want to stop," she mumbled. Then she heard a snap near her ear, and suddenly she was wide awake. Geti had to squint as she looked up because the sun was already high in the sky, but through the glare she could see she was in big trouble.

Geti jumped up but Cushman was ready for her. He had snapped a collar made of metal links around her neck while she was asleep, and held on to it with a leash. When Geti tried to pull away, the collar tightened painfully around her neck. It prevented her from struggling; she had to follow Cushman's commands.

"Let's go," he said. "No shenanigans from you, ya hear me?"

Cushman didn't say anything else as they walked, but Geti noticed a happy bounce to his steps. She didn't panic; she knew the smug, victorious look would disappear from his face as soon as she found the opportunity to say the magic words and return to Dog Park.

Cushman led Geti to a cage located in the shadow of a supply shed behind the zoo, far from the flowering bushes and willowy trees where visitors were welcome. None of the other animals were nearby. He opened the cage door, knelt down, and shoved her in. His big belly blocked the cage opening while he removed the leash. Then he quickly shut the door, and Geti heard the lock click into place.

"Rest up today, my friend," Cushman said. "Tomorrow we'll begin our work." With that, he left and Geti was alone.

Chapter Eight

Introducing Arabella

AFTER CUSHMAN left, Geti took a moment to examine her new surroundings. She had only enough room in the cage to take a few steps in each direction, and the ceiling was barely two inches above her head. Mouse droppings and a lumpy, musty mat filled with sawdust covered the hard floor. A dead fly floated in a bowl of water that she supposed was meant for her to drink. Through the bars she could see a chain link fence, off in the distance, separating her from the rest of the zoo. She couldn't see the other animals, but their odors wafted through the air.

Geti wanted this adventure to end. She couldn't wait to get home. She closed her eyes and as quickly as she could, she said:

"To Norumbega
In days long past
Where memories made
Will forever last.
Then home again
Where I belong
But in my heart
Norumbega's song."

Something was wrong; Geti was still in the cage. The poem didn't sound right. A word, a sentence, perhaps? Something was misplaced. She was still so sleepy from dancing all night, and rattled by her encounter with Cushman; she just couldn't think straight. She repeated the poem a few more times, but she knew she wasn't remembering it correctly.

There had to be another way out of this cage. Maybe she could find someone to help her.

"Hello?" she called out hopefully. When no one answered, she barked much louder. "Hello! Is anyone out there?"

Again there was no reply. She was penned too far from the walking paths. There was no one nearby to hear her cries for help.

Suddenly Geti felt a surge of relief. Of course! *In times long past!* She had been using the word 'days' instead of 'times.' Now she was sure of the rhyme.

She shut her eyes tightly again and shouted:

"To Norumbega
In times long past
Where memories made
Will forever last.
Then home again
Where I belong

But in my heart
Norumbega's song."

Before Geti even opened her eyes, she knew she was still trapped. There was no magic in this cage. Hadn't the frog warned her of this? "Don't get caught by Cushman," he had said. "If you do, you'll never get home. The poem will only work if you're free." That's what he had told her, and he had been right.

Over and over, Geti repeated the rhyme, but it was useless. Now she was truly scared, and she felt more alone than she thought possible. She lay down on the bed of musty sawdust and waited for the day to pass.

Cushman came to the cage once more that day, to bring Geti some food. "Eat it," he instructed. "You'll need your strength." But she felt ill and didn't go near the bowl. Things only got worse when he said to her, "Your name is Arabella now. Get used to it."

When darkness fell, the music of Norumbega began to play. Geti tried to recapture the thrill she had felt on the previous night outside the ballroom. She danced and twirled as well as she could within the confines of her cage, but the music couldn't conquer her despair. Even while she danced, Geti never stopped saying the magic words, though she had lost faith that they would ever return her to Dog Park.

Chapter Nine

Star of the Show

CUSHMAN RETURNED to the cage early the next morning, just after dawn. "Rise and shine, Arabella," he said, as he attached the leash to the metal collar around her neck. "It's time to make you a star."

They walked over to the fenced-in stage where Geti had seen Cushman perform with the white horses. He opened the gate and they stepped inside. Geti watched with dismay as he shut the gate tightly behind him and double-checked the latch. Her escape route was blocked.

"OK, Arabella," he said. "Now let's see how smart you really are. The faster you learn the routines, the better it'll be for you."

The six white horses were already on the stage. Cushman led Geti onto it, and unsnapped the leash. "Stay," he commanded.

Geti could feel six pairs of eyes studying her from top to bottom. When Cushman stepped off the stage and walked over to a bin to fetch his equipment, she turned to the horses. She hoped they would be friendly; she desperately needed an ally.

"Hi," she said enthusiastically.

None of the horses answered. The tallest one turned his back to Geti when she spoke. One by one, the other five horses turned too. Geti looked at the six swishing tails in confusion.

"Hey!" she said, and because she didn't know what else to say, she said, "I'm Geti."

"LIAR." The tallest horse turned back to face her, and all the other horses followed their leader.

"Liar," he said again. "Your name is Arabella." The other horses took up the chorus.

"Liar, Liar, Liar," they whinnied. They all swished their tails back and forth as they said the words.

Geti cowered and stepped backward. Had she taken one more step, she would have fallen off the stage, but a shot rang out. "Quiet!" Cushman yelled, and Geti realized the noise was the sound of his whip snapping in the air.

The animals fell silent. Cushman turned back to his equipment bin.

Geti faced the horses. "What's your problem?" she whispered crossly.

The tall horse scowled for a moment and flattened his ears. He gave two snorts before he hissed, "Just who do you think you are, you... you... dog?" Foam sprayed out of his mouth as he angrily spat the words. "We've been working on this stage for years, and now you think you're the star of the show? Well, think again."

"No, you've got it all backward," Geti cried. "I don't even want to be here!"

This seemed to be the wrong thing to say to the horse. He grew even angrier.

"Why not?" he demanded to know. "Aren't we good enough for you? Are you afraid we won't remember our steps, and we'll make you look bad? I wouldn't be so high and mighty if I were you. We're professional entertainers. What stage experience have you had? Clearly none at all."

Geti's eyes filled with tears as she realized it would be useless to appeal to the horses for help. She tried to ignore their hurtful words, and pay attention to Cushman and his commands.

All that morning and the next, Cushman showed Geti what to do. At first, the routines were easy. She had to jump over the shortest horse, and scoot under the tallest one. She had to sit on the back of the broadest horse as he trotted around the stage. Though she worried the horses might trip her up, they didn't dare misstep while Cushman carried his whip.

When she had mastered those tricks, Cushman worked with Geti alone and taught her to jump through a large hoop. He made her do it over, and over, and over again until she could do it perfectly, without a single one of her long silky hairs touching the edges.

The tasks got more complicated on the third day. Cushman erected six wooden steps with a platform at the top. He set up the large hoop at the same height as the platform. Geti had to jump off the platform, through the hoop, and land on a soft mat below. When she perfected that routine, he added more steps to raise the height of the platform, then raised the height of the hoop to match, and moved them a little farther apart. He also marked an X with chalk on the mat. She had to spring off the high platform, fly through the middle of the hoop, and land precisely on the X. It was difficult,

and hard on her legs when she landed, but her aim improved with each attempt.

They practiced until mid-morning each day, when Cushman brought Geti back to her cage. Exhausted, she spent the afternoons catching up on her sleep.

Mazie, the trapeze artist who had dangled from the high wire over the river, brought Geti her dinner each evening. This quickly became the highlight of Geti's day. Mazie would feed her and walk her on the leash outside the cage. She would gently brush Geti's long fur and speak kindly to her.

"He's not really a bad sort," Mazie said to Geti about Cushman. "He's worried about his job, that's all. He's afraid he'll get fired if he doesn't improve the act."

Geti didn't care at all about Cushman's job. But she wanted Mazie to keep coming back, and snuggled into her lap for comfort.

Late one afternoon, voices woke Geti from her nap.

"She seems to be doing pretty well," Geti heard Mazie say.

"Yup, that dog has lotsa spunk," Cushman replied. "Pretty soon she'll be ready for the real thing."

"You're really going to set the hoop on fire?" asked Mazie.

"Sure! We'll give it a test run in a few days. Can't ya

picture it? The horse will be galloping 'round the stage. Arabella, with that fiery red hair of hers, will come flyin' through the flamin' hoop and land with perfect timing on the horse's back. The audience is gonna love it."

"Have you seen Arabella dance?" Mazie asked. "I watch her sometimes late at night, dancing in her cage. She's really good, you know. Fun to watch. An audience would love that even more. Why don't you have her dance on stage, instead of jumping through fire?"

"Nah," said Cushman.

"I hope you know what you're doing," Mazie warned.

And Geti, in shock at what she had overheard, let out a long, slow moan. For the first time since her long ordeal began, she felt defeated. Cushman had won.

Chapter Ten

Murphy in Frog Park

BACK IN Dog Park, Murphy was worried and missed Geti terribly.

Geti had been gone for six days, and Murphy spent most of that time sitting by the river feeling regretful. She was sorry she hadn't believed Geti could really hear musical magic. (Or was it magical music?) She was sorry she hadn't paid attention to anything the frog said. Most of all, she was sorry that wherever Geti was, she was alone.

Murphy knew Geti well enough to know she would never stay away from Dog Park for this long unless something terrible had happened. But she just could not imagine what that terrible thing might be.

She stopped playing with the other dogs. She spent her days trying to find the frog that had taught Geti the magic words, but every frog she approached either looked at her with confusion or hopped away.

One day, as she was starting to feel hopeless, she noticed some sounds out on the water.

♪ croak ♪ croak ♪ croak ♪ ♪cccrroakkk♪

It was the sweetest song Murphy had ever heard.

"Frog, hey, Frog!" she yelled.

"Oh, it's you. What's the matter? Is my singing bothering you again? I'd rather talk to your friend. Where's your friend?" the frog croaked in reply.

"Exactly! Where is my friend?" Murphy cried. Her eyes followed the sound of the raspy voice and finally spotted the frog sunning himself on a floating log.

"How would I know? Is she lost?" he asked.

"I don't know. I was hoping you could tell me. You're the one that sent her to.... to... whatever it's called."

"Norumbega?"

"Yes, that place! I think she went to… to… that place, and she never came home again."

"Maybe she likes it there," said the frog. "Maybe she likes the music."

"No! No, no, no. Geti would never stay away this long without telling me, without talking to me. Something's wrong! Very, very wrong," Murphy insisted.

"Uh-oh," replied the frog.

Murphy's heart sank. Nothing good ever follows the words "uh-oh."

"Uh-oh, what?" she asked.

"Uh-oh, Cushman," he replied. "I knew this wasn't going to work out well. I knew it was a mistake to teach the words to a dog."

"What in the world is a Cushman?" Panic was creeping into Murphy's voice.

The frog leaped from his log onto the shore, and hopped over to Murphy. It's hard to read a frog's facial expressions, but Murphy thought she saw a look of concern flicker across his face.

"There's nothing I can do for your friend," the frog said. "If you want to try to help her, you'll have to go to Norumbega yourself."

"And just how do you propose I do that?" Murphy asked.

"Say the magic words, like the other dog did," was the reply.

"But I don't know the words," Murphy explained.

"You were right there when I taught them to your friend." The frog sighed. "Never mind," he said. "I'll teach them to you again. Close your eyes and repeat each line after me.

"To Norumbega in times long past," the frog said.

And Murphy said, "To Morungeba in times long past."

"No!" said the frog. "Pay attention. To Norumbega in times long past."

And Murphy said, "To Burgonema in times long past."

There were a few seconds of silence. Not sure what to expect next, Murphy opened her eyes. The frog was just staring at her, shaking his head.

"Okay," he finally said. "Let's go to Plan B."

"There's a Plan B?" echoed Murphy with relief.

"I guess I'll have to take you to Norumbega myself," said the frog. He explained to Murphy that as long as they were touching or connected in some way, only one of them needed to say the magic words.

"But there are going to be some conditions," said the frog, puffing his chest out in a self-important way.

"Condition Number One: I'm just dropping you off.

I'm not going to stay to help you find your friend. If you can't rescue her, you're going to have to find your own way home. Is that understood?"

"Yes," said Murphy.

"Condition Number Two: If you ever return to Dog Park, I never want to hear you say that frogs are foolish or silly."

"Of course," promised Murphy.

"Condition Number Three: If you do return safely, I never want to hear you refer to this park as 'Dog Park' again. Henceforth, it will be known as 'Frog Park'."

"Um, okay," said Murphy.

Now the frog was clearly enjoying himself. "Condition Number Four: From now on, when you hear me singing, you must join in and sing along."

"Well, now you've just gone too far!" Murphy protested.

"Relax! I didn't think you'd agree to that one. Don't get yourself in a dither. Just stand still. I'm coming aboard."

With one great leap, the frog landed squarely on her back, and then hung on precariously as Murphy jiggled and fidgeted impatiently.

"I'm sitting on a dog. I must be crazy," the frog muttered. But he kept his part of their agreement; he closed his eyes and recited the magic words:

"To Norumbega
In times long past
Where memories made
Will forever last.
Then home again
Where I belong
But in my heart
Norumbega's song."

And just like that, Murphy and the frog were standing at the edge of the river in Norumbega Park.

Chapter Eleven

A Visit from Trixie

MURPHY OPENED her eyes when she heard the frog croak, "Hey! Pay attention. Go find your friend."

Murphy gasped. "It <u>is</u> real," she exclaimed, as she looked around at the colorful boats and all the people lining the shore. "Geti was right all along. The magic is real."

"Of course it's real. What did you think? Goodbye, Dog. I'm going home." The frog closed his eyes.

"No, wait!" yelled Murphy. "Where will I find her? What do I need to know?"

"That other dog is probably somewhere in the zoo. Cushman is in charge of the zoo. You need to stay away from Cushman. You have quite a challenge ahead of you, I'd say. Good luck."

"Where is the zoo? How can I get her out? How will I recognize Cushman?" Murphy cried. But it was too late. The frog would not let her distract him from reciting his charmed poem, and when he said the final word, he disappeared.

Murphy took a deep breath. Geti needed her, and she would do anything to help her best friend. *Focus*, she coached herself. *Focus and figure out a plan.*

She examined her surroundings. She edged toward a family who appeared to be moving on from the river, picking up their towels and putting on their shoes.

Murphy made a quick decision to follow them and see where they were headed. Maybe they would eventually lead her to the zoo.

As she trailed behind the family, there were moments when Murphy almost forgot her mission. There was so much to look at! She stayed close by while the three children rode on the Ferris wheel, and their father won a stuffed bunny by shooting a water gun at brightly painted wooden ducks. She hovered behind them while the family watched a clown twist balloons into hats for the children to wear, and into shapes that looked like giraffes and swans. Next they followed a path to a dazzling fountain, which had jets of water cascading over multi-colored lights.

When it was time to eat, the family led the way to a picnic area where the children played on a huge wooden swing wide enough for all three of them to sit together. The parents laid out a blanket and lunch food, while Murphy lay down to wait in the shade of a tree, which felt familiar and comforting.

A man approached. He knelt down in front of her, his big belly hanging almost to the ground, and scratched her behind her floppy ears and under her chin.

"Hey there, pretty dog," he said. He called over to the family sitting nearby. "Is this your dog?" he asked.

"No, she seems to be a stray," the father answered.

"Not anymore," the man murmured, and smiled. The hand patting Murphy's head suddenly grabbed the nape of her neck. Murphy jerked her head but the man clung on.

"No!" Murphy yowled.

"Let her go, Cushman. She's my dog." A woman had come walking up the path, and now she stood in front of Cushman with her arms sternly crossed.

"You and I both know you don't own a dog, Mazie. She's a stray."

"No, that's my dog, Trixie. I brought her with me this morning, but she wandered away from me when my back was turned. Let her go, you'll see."

Grudgingly, Cushman released his hold on Murphy, while Mazie snapped her fingers and called, "Here, Trixie. Come."

Murphy bounded over to Mazie. She leaped in the air, trying to cover Mazie's face with kisses.

"Good girl, Trixie. Calm down now. Don't leave me again, you hear?" Mazie smiled sweetly at Murphy and then at Cushman, who scowled at her in return.

"Keep an eye on your dog, Mazie. Don't let her wander around here alone," Cushman warned as the woman and dog hurried away. "You never know what could happen to her."

Chapter Twelve

Behind the Zoo

MURPHY STAYED glued to her new friend's side. Mazie carried a pile of large posters advertising the many shows in the park, and together they strolled around Norumbega while she handed them out and chatted with everyone they met. "Come see my amazing high-wire act at the river tonight! You won't believe your eyes," Mazie would tell them, or "Don't miss the vaudeville show at eight o'clock. It's the funniest revue we've ever put on!" Sometimes she said, "The Ozzie Nelson Band is appearing at the ballroom tonight. Put on your dancing shoes!" and occasionally she reminded them, "Cushman's Animal Show performs twice a day, at noon and four o'clock."

When she ran out of posters, Mazie turned to Murphy and said, "Our next job is to feed Arabella. You'll like each other, I bet."

At first, Murphy didn't realize they were heading toward the zoo. But her heart began to flutter as the stench of the large animals reached her nose, and it struck her that Geti might be among them.

Then Mazie turned onto a path that led to an area behind the zoo. "Arabella's over this way," she said, opening a gate in a chain link fence. Murphy hesitated. She couldn't bear to miss a chance to find her friend.

"Trixie, come! Believe me, you don't want to go into the zoo. You might run right into Cushman."

Murphy realized she would never be able to rescue Geti if Cushman had them both locked up. Unsure of her best course of action, she reluctantly followed Mazie beyond the chain link fence.

As they walked away from the zoo, its smells faded slightly, and Murphy began to pick up a new scent. After a few more steps, it grew stronger and Murphy broke into a run.

"Trixie! Come back!" Mazie shouted. But she had no need to worry. She found Murphy at Geti's cage, the

two dogs nose to nose through the bars, speaking to each other in high-pitched squeals while their bodies wiggled with emotion.

"Ah," Mazie said. "You two already know each other, don't you? This is why you're here, Trixie."

Mazie picked up the leash, which was lying on the ground. She opened the cage door and attached the leash to Geti's collar. "I wish I could let you go free, Arabella, but I just can't. I'd get fired from my job for sure. But at least you can be close to your friend for a while.

Even with the leash constraining Geti's movements, she and Murphy managed to roll and wrestle and mouth each other with affection. Neither of them could believe they were together again.

But after just a few minutes, Mazie said, "I have to get ready for my trapeze act now. I'm sorry, Arabella. You need to go back into your cage. It's time for Trixie and me to leave."

Not knowing what else to do, Geti obediently returned to her cage. But Murphy would have none of it. She stubbornly sat down and refused to come when Mazie called.

"Please, Trixie, come with me. I hate to think about what would happen if Cushman finds you here."

In response to that, Murphy took a leap and hurled herself on top of Geti's cage. She lied down on it, draping her body over as much of the cage as she could.

Mazie sighed. "I understand," she said. "You're not going to leave your friend." Then she focused her attention on Geti.

"Cushman will be here even earlier in the morning than usual, Arabella. He, well, he has some new things he wants to teach you. If you care about Trixie, make sure she's gone before the sun rises. I'll leave the gate in the chain link fence open so she can get out."

Mazie reached over and caressed the fur on Murphy's head. "Good luck, girls, and be careful," she said as she left.

Murphy jumped down. She looked at Geti. "*Arabella?*" she asked.

"*Trixie?*" Geti replied. And they both began to laugh.

Their lightheartedness did not last long, however. For the next several hours, they shared stories of everything that had happened since they had last seen one another. Later in the evening, when the music from the ballroom began to play, Geti stood up and danced. It was the first time Murphy had ever heard the music, and she began to dance too. They twirled, and Murphy leaped and pirouetted outside of the cage. She finally understood the rapture Geti had always found in the music.

When they were too tired to dance any longer, Murphy caught her breath and said to Geti, "I'm so sorry I never believed you."

They both cried as Geti told Murphy about Cushman's plans. "Even if I get through the fire safely," she said, "that horse will never let me land on him. He'll speed up or slow down and I'll crash to the ground without a mat to soften my fall."

"How are we going to get you out of here?" Murphy wailed. "I wish… I wish I could somehow open the lock on your cage."

Geti stopped sobbing and thought hard for a moment. Smiling brightly at her best friend, she exclaimed, "Oh Murphy, you're a genius!"

Chapter Thirteen

In the Dark

GETI AND Murphy spent a long time ironing out every detail of their plan.

"You'll have to be very, very quiet," Geti warned. "You don't want to do anything that attracts Cushman's attention."

"Won't people see me? Won't they see the bear leaving his cage?" Murphy asked.

"Every part of the park is closed late at night except for the ballroom. That's where all the people are right now," Geti explained. "And Dune has escaped lots of times. He'll know what to do. Besides, it's a cloudy night so there's no moonlight; you two will be hidden by the darkness as long as you're quiet and stay away from the music."

When they had everything thought out, and had gone over their plan one final time, Murphy rose to leave.

"I'll be back in a few minutes, Geti. Then we'll go home."

"Be careful, Murphy. I'll never forgive myself if something happens to you."

Just as Mazie had promised, the gate in the chain link fence was open. Murphy slipped out and followed her nose to the zoo.

A mixture of smells immediately assaulted her at the entrance. The combination of lions and bears, monkeys and zebras, moose and buffalo created an odor that made Murphy's stomach clench with anxiety. She paused when she remembered that she had never met a bear; she couldn't identify which scent belonged to Dune. She shuddered at the thought of wandering through the darkness of the zoo, looking for him. But she soldiered on.

She padded silently up one path and down another, peering into cages of animals she had never imagined she'd see. Even in their sleep, they looked powerful and dangerous. A few stirred as she passed. One lion opened his eyes, and Murphy froze in her tracks. She was sure he could hear her heart beating. But the lion simply readjusted his position and was snoring softly again within moments.

Finally Murphy arrived at the biggest cage of all, the den that housed four bears. Now she was faced with a new problem: How was she going to wake Dune without waking the others?

"Dune?" she called softly through the bars of the cage. There was no response. Bears are known for sleeping very soundly.

She tried again a bit louder. "Dune?"

Some of the animals in other cages were beginning to rustle and murmur, but the bears slept on.

"Dune," she said even louder, and then even louder still, "DUNE!"

Now the bears were awake, along with all the animals in the adjacent cages. There was a great deal of growling and roaring. The monkeys screeched and rattled the bars of their cage.

"Who are you? Don't bother us. What do you want? Go away." The bears all growled at once, and Murphy could barely make herself heard in the uproar.

A pen of white horses began buzzing with activity. The horses neighed and whinnied. They held their heads high and pinned back their ears. The largest horse began to kick the dirt beneath his front hooves, and then the other horses kicked dirt, too.

"Dune! Is one of you named Dune?" Murphy yelled into the bear den.

The largest bear stepped forward. "I'm Dune," he said, and he signaled to the other bears to quiet down. The animals in the surrounding cages slowly settled back into their sleep too. Only the horses kept up a racket.

"What do you want?" asked Dune.

"I'm here for Geti," Murphy whispered. "Geti needs your help."

Dune looked perplexed for a moment. He shook his head hard as though to fight off his drowsiness and think more clearly. Then his face brightened.

"G-G-G-Geti?" he exclaimed.

As quickly as she could, Murphy explained Geti's situation. Dune immediately understood what he needed to do. "I'll be out of here in a jiffy," he assured Murphy.

But as the bear fiddled with the lock on his cage, the horses grew more agitated. "It's a dog, another dog," the ringleader neighed, and his followers took up the cry. "A dog! A dog!" they whinnied.

The horses' ruckus woke the other animals again. The commotion in the zoo grew louder and louder.

"Hurry! Before someone comes!" Murphy cried.

"Here we go!" yelled Dune as he swung the cage door open and stepped out. Murphy noticed gratefully that he shut the door behind him, keeping the other bears securely locked in.

Together they raced to Geti's cage, where Dune gave her a hearty, "Hello, G-G-G-Geti!" before he started to tackle her lock.

Geti had a lot to say while Dune concentrated on his task.

"Murphy, you did it! You found Dune! And Dune, I'm so grateful you're helping me. I was so worried. I could hear all that noise coming from the zoo. Those horses! And roaring, and other sounds. Whoa!" She jabbered on and on to calm her nerves. Murphy, meanwhile, paced silently.

Suddenly, Murphy said, "Shhhh! Listen."

The three friends froze. Far off in the distance, they heard Cushman's voice. "Dune, Dune boy, where are you?"

Someone else yelled, "Is he in the tree?"

"No," Cushman shouted. "I already looked there. Dune! Where are you?"

"Will you get into trouble for helping me?" Geti asked Dune worriedly.

"Nah, that won't be a problem. I have a plan! I

snuck out of my cage, and I can sneak back in. The next time anyone looks, I'll be back in my bed, fast asleep. Cushman will think he only imagined I was missing. Ha Ha!" Dune let out a loud guffaw.

"SHHHH!" both dogs warned.

"Dune! Where are you?" Cushman's voice was traveling in the direction of Geti's cage. "Dune, where are ya hiding, buddy?"

"Hurry!" Murphy yelled to Dune. But the bear remained unflappable.

"Wahoo!" he exclaimed just a moment later. He ceremoniously opened the cage door, and Geti leaped out.

"How can I ever thank you?" she cried.

"Well, if you ever have the opportunity, please bring me some ice cream. I'd like that a lot!"

Laughing as always, Dune lumbered off toward the zoo. Geti ran alongside him, until they reached the chain link fence.

"Thank you again, Dune," she called after him.

"Goodbye, G-G-G-Geti," he called over his shoulder. "See if you can find some pistachio or strawberry."

THUD! THUD! THUD! Geti was starting to feel the vibration of Cushman's footsteps.

"He's coming!" she shrieked to Murphy. "Say the magic words."

"But…"

"Quickly!" she screamed. She closed her eyes, and the rhyme poured from her lips in a great gush:

"To Norumbega
In times long past
Where memories made
Will forever last.
Then home again
Where I belong
But in my heart
Norumbega's song."

Geti concentrated so hard on the poem she didn't hear Murphy yell, "But Geti, I don't know the words!"

Murphy ran toward Geti to grab hold of her, but it was too late.

Geti was gone.

Chapter Fourteen

The Call of the Magic

GETI DID not need to open her eyes to know she was home. The stillness of the night was broken only by crickets chirping in the tall grass, and leaves rustling in the gentle breeze. The fragrances of the flowers growing wild in Dog Park made her gasp with joy. Tranquility settled around her like a cozy blanket. Geti knew she would never leave Dog Park again.

"You did it, Murphy! You rescued me. You may have saved my life!"

Geti opened her eyes and turned to look for her

friend. But Murphy wasn't next to her, nor was she behind Geti, nor off to the side, nor off in the distance. Murphy was nowhere to be seen. Geti was alone.

The realization of what she had done almost knocked Geti to the ground. Now she remembered Murphy describing how the frog had sat on her back, transporting her to Norumbega. Murphy hadn't learned the magic words. She had risked her life to save Geti, and Geti had repaid Murphy by leaving her behind.

A vision of her friend locked in Cushman's cage stormed its way into Geti's mind. "Murphy!" she cried as loud as her voice would allow, as though it might somehow carry to Norumbega and let her friend know help was on the way.

In an equally loud voice, she hollered:

"To Norumbega
In times long past
Where memories made
Will forever last.
Then home again
Where I belong
But in my heart
Norumbega's song."

An instant later Geti was back at the spot she had

just escaped with Murphy's help. She immediately saw the cage was empty, but before she could enjoy even a moment of relief, she noticed the leash that had been on the ground was missing. Murphy was missing too.

"Murph?" Geti whispered. She spun around as something crackled, then saw it was just a squirrel scurrying over some dried leaves on the ground. The fur on her neck stood at attention; she wondered if Cushman might be lurking in the darkness, waiting for the right moment to grab her. What if he had his whip?

Geti's thoughts whizzed around in a frightened jumble. Where was Murphy? Had she run back into the zoo, looking for Dune? Or could she be in the park, searching for Mazie? Would she have found her way to the river, hoping to escape to the other side? Worst of all: Did Cushman catch her and take her somewhere else? She could barely think straight as she considered the possibilities, all the while knowing time might be running out.

♪ ♪ bbbʀʀʀʀuuummmppp ♪ ♪

The music was playing in the ballroom. It was distracting Geti from thinking. She tried to block it out but she couldn't. It seemed louder than usual. It was insistent. She tossed her head to shake it away but that only seemed to make the music more powerful. It almost seemed like the music was calling out to her.

That was it! The music was calling out to her! Geti knew exactly where to find Murphy.

The clouds overhead parted, making way for the sparkling night sky, and the music guided Geti's feet. She ran faster than she had ever run before, almost flying just above the ground, never hesitating at the forks as one moonlit path crisscrossed with another, and then another.

When the ballroom was in her sight, Geti skidded to a stop. Was she too late?

There they were, Murphy and Cushman, just outside the ballroom. Geti understood that Murphy had run toward the music and the people, but Cushman had caught up with her. He held one end of the leash, and had somehow managed to loop the other end around Murphy's neck. He was pulling and tugging Murphy with both hands, but hadn't anticipated her strength. She had no intention of letting him drag her back to the cage, and she pulled in the opposite direction with equal determination.

They were intent on their struggle; neither of them noticed Geti's return. Quietly she snuck up behind Cushman, opened her mouth wide, took aim, and...

"YEOW!" Cushman yelled as Geti's teeth tore through his pants and settled firmly into the flesh just below the back of his knee. But amazingly, he did not let go of the leash. He continued to pull, Murphy continued to resist, and Geti hung on to Cushman's calf with all the power her jaw could muster.

Several people who had come out of the ballroom for a breath of fresh air stood nearby and watched the struggle. "Do ya think one of you can help me here?" Cushman yelled to them. "Get this dog off my leg!"

No one stepped forward to assist Cushman. They seemed unsure about who really needed help the most.

Cushman kicked his leg out as hard as he could. Geti lost her grip as she was knocked a few feet into the air. She immediately lunged again, but Cushman was ready for her this time. He wiggled and waved his leg back and forth to prevent her from grabbing on. She tried, but the best she could do was to grab the bottom of his pants.

She pulled on the pant leg as hard as she could, hoping to make him lose his balance. But Cushman was like a tree planted firmly in the ground. She could not get him to topple.

More people were gathering to watch the scuffle. "Pull harder!" she heard Murphy yell, and Geti felt a surge of energy. She gave the pant leg a huge tug.

POP!

One of Cushman's red suspenders popped right off his pants. When Geti saw that, she pulled again, even harder.

POP!

The second suspender popped open.

His waistband had been resting below his big belly, and with nothing holding them up, Cushman's pants sank slowly to the ground.

The spectators burst into laughter, pointing at the man standing in his underwear with his pants puddled around his shoes. Cushman scowled and snarled, "Get this mutt offa me!"

Geti still hung on to his pants, trying to make him trip and fall. Cushman managed to remain upright and he held on to the leash as tightly as before. "Hey, can somebody give me a hand here?" he shouted once again, this time in a pleading voice.

The laughter died down. Finally, a man stepped forward to help him.

Just as the fellow reached for her, Geti let go of Cushman's pants. She jumped away to avoid being grabbed.

♪♪bbbRRRuuummmppp♪♪

The music played on, louder than ever. Geti understood what she needed to do.

She began to dance.

"GETI!" Murphy cried. "WHAT ARE YOU DOING?"

"Hang on, Murphy," Geti shouted. But that's all she said, because she needed to save her breath for her performance.

Then Geti danced like she had never danced before.

She leaped, she twirled, she pirouetted, she somersaulted. She spun, she sashayed. She balanced on her hind legs and swung into the Mambo, the Cha Cha, the Jitterbug, the Lindy Hop. The magical music was in control of her limbs, moving her in ways she never knew she could move.

More people gathered outside, watching in awe. They began to applaud Geti and cheer her on. One person yelled, "Hey, Mister, why don't ya let the dogs go?"

"Yeah," someone else yelled. "Let the dogs go!"

The audience grew bigger. More people came out of the ballroom to watch Geti dance. They formed a circle around her, clapping their hands and stomping their feet in rhythm with the music and Geti's movements. Some boaters docked their canoes and came to watch. The park employees left their posts and joined the pack.

More and more people yelled, "Let the dogs go!" and it became a cry they shouted in harmony:

"LET THE DOGS GO! LET THE DOGS GO!"

The noise outside attracted the attention of even more people in the ballroom. They continued to stream from the building to see what was happening. Soon the ballroom had completely emptied. The hundreds of dancers were followed by all the musicians, still playing their instruments as if they were in a marching band. The tuba players, the trombonists, the saxophonists, the trumpeters joined the group surrounding Geti. The rousing music blared while Geti continued to dance. Now she was soaring even higher, spinning even faster. The shouts from the swelling throng of people grew louder and more demanding.

"LET THE DOGS GO! LET THE DOGS GO!"

"LET THE DOGS GO! LET THE DOGS GO!"

Blood was trickling from Cushman's leg. His pants were tangled around his ankles. His face was very white and his eyes were huge. Still, he hung on to the leash with all his strength as Murphy continued to struggle.

A woman emerged from the crowd. It was Mazie. She approached Cushman and put her hand on his wrist. In a gentle voice, she said, "Give me the leash, Cushman. It's time to let the dogs go."

Cushman looked stunned and was staring at the excited mob with confusion, as though he couldn't make sense of where he was or what was happening.

He jerked his arm away from Mazie. "No," he said hoarsely and tried to back away, but finally tripped over his pants and landed squarely on his bottom.

The leash was still in Cushman's hand. He studied it for a minute. Then, meekly, he reached up and handed it to Mazie.

Everyone erupted in cheers and whistles as Mazie unwound the leash from Murphy's neck. "Let's go help your friend," she said.

The music played on, and the men and women began to dance under the moonlight. In the midst of them all, Geti was still twirling and leaping.

"Geti, you can stop!" Murphy cried. "We're free!"

When she heard those words, the spell of the music was broken and Geti collapsed in a heap. Her body suddenly ached with exhaustion. "Free!" She panted. "Free!"

Mazie knelt by Geti's side and removed the metal collar from her neck. "You're quite a pair of dogs," she said as she kissed them both on the top of their heads and then on their snouts. "I'm so glad I got to know you, and I won't ever forget you. Goodbye, Arabella. Goodbye, Trixie. No one will stop you from going home now."

"We're free! We're going home!" Murphy sang happily, doing her own little dance in circles around Geti. She remembered to add, "I'll have to hold on to you while you say those magic words!"

Murphy picked up Geti's tail in her mouth and clamped on firmly. A small wince escaped from Geti's lips but then she quickly said, "Don't let go! We need to stay together."

Geti pulled herself up onto wobbly legs. She looked around one last time at the things she loved about Norumbega: the dancers, the musicians, and Mazie. She thought of the bear that had helped her, and hoped he was soundly asleep in his bed. Then she allowed herself one final look at Cushman. He had gotten himself off the ground, pulled up his pants, and was holding them in place with both hands while he limped away from the ballroom as fast as he could manage. Geti had a feeling he might keep walking, right past the zoo and out through the Norumbega exit, never to return.

She smiled at Murphy, shut her eyes tightly, and found enough breath to say the words that would take the two friends home:

> "To Norumbega
> In times long past
> Where memories made
> Will forever last.
> Then home again
> Where I belong
> But in my heart
> Norumbega's song."

Chapter Fifteen

Under the Moon

AFTER THEY escaped from Norumbega and settled back into their lives at Dog Park, Murphy asked only one thing of Geti. She asked that Geti never mention music or magic again.

Geti was happy to make that promise.

In the days, and months, and years that followed, Geti never talked about the magical music. When she heard it calling to her, she did her best to ignore it. She played in the river with the other dogs, joining in when they swam, and chased geese, and fetched sticks. She wrestled, and rolled, and raced in the field, and never gave up in games of tug-of-war. She didn't look for the frog that had taught her the magic poem. Once, when she heard him singing, she ran up the hill and kept going until his croaks had completely drifted away.

Over time, Geti forgot some of the magic words, just enough to make the rhyme useless. All the other dogs (except Murphy) eventually forgot that Geti once had a reputation for being rather strange.

But Geti had a small secret that she never shared, not even with Murphy. Especially not with Murphy.

Every now and then, on very rare occasions, not very often at all, when the moon was bright and the air was still, and all the other creatures in the park were asleep, Geti would sit by the river and wait for the music. When it started to softly ripple across the water, she would remember how it felt to dance outside the ballroom. She would remember how the instruments sounded, lifting her with joy. The music would grow loud in her mind, and she could hear each trumpet, each trombone, and each drum beat.

On those rare nights, under the glow of the moon, Geti would spin, and leap, and pirouette. She would twirl and she would somersault. She would dance until her legs could barely hold her up, until she was entirely spent. Then Geti would snuggle beneath the sheltering branches of the copper beech tree, and sleep safely and happily. When her friends arrived in the morning, Geti was ready for another day in Dog Park.

Author's Note

NORUMBEGA PARK was a nationally renowned amusement park, which operated in the Auburndale neighborhood of Newton, Massachusetts from 1897 until 1963. It was among the best of the "trolley parks" built across the country at the turn of the century to attract streetcar riders on the weekends.

While Cushman is a completely fictional character, in most other ways I've tried to accurately describe Norumbega and its charm during the late 1930s and early 1940s. I've also taken the liberty of including a few of the park's notable attractions from other decades, even if they no longer existed by the time this story takes place.

Amid lush lawns and flowering gardens, Norumbega housed New England's biggest zoo and its ice-cream loving bear, featured an "iron-jaw" acrobat named Mazie who dangled over the river from a high wire, offered paddle boat and canoe rides, hosted a women's softball team, and proudly showcased a magnificent carousel and Ferris wheel. The park was best known for its Totem Pole Ballroom, which routinely attracted bands like Benny Goodman's and Tommy Dorsey's, singers like Frank Sinatra and Dinah Shore, and hundreds of couples who danced to their music each weekend.

Today, most of the land that was once home to the original Norumbega Park is the site of a large hotel. One section of about thirteen acres, alongside the Charles River, has been set aside as conservation land. Also named Norumbega, it has aged into an overgrown field whose lush, natural beauty will always be protected. It is enjoyed regularly by local residents and their dogs, and is affectionately known as "Dog Park."

For more information about Norumbega's history, visit www.magicnorumbega.com

Boating on the Charles River at Norumbega Park
was an extremely popular pastime.

Circa 1940

Animal acts and mechanical rides drew large crowds to Norumbega Park.

Tillie the Elephant, 1928

Ferris Wheel 1928 - 1938

The Caterpillar

Norumbega Postcard, 1907

Norumbega's bears were the zoo's main attraction,
but the carousel animals were also impressive.

Photos courtesy of Historic Newton, Newton, MA and Remember Productions

Mazie Lunette wowed the crowds at
Norumbega Park with her iron-jaw trapeze act, *1924*

"The Totem Pole Belles" *circa 1940*
Norumbega women's professional softball team

The Totem Pole (*1930-1964*) was known as
"America's Most Beautiful Ballroom."

totem pole=

takes pleasure in presenting

GUY LOMBARDO

FOR 4 NIGHTS

Wednesday, March 26	**$1.75**	Per Couple Including Tax
Thursday, March 27		
Friday, March 28	**$2.40**	Per Couple Including Tax
Saturday, March 29		

Tickets now on sale at JORDAN MARSH TRAVEL BUREAU
and at NORUMBEGA PARK

Coming soon: TEX BENEKE and the GLENN MILLER ORCHESTRA
also EDDY HOWARD and his Orchestra

DANCING EVERY
WED., FRI. and SAT.
THROUGHOUT THE
WINTER SEASON

NORUMBEGA PARK
Auburndale (Newton), Mass.

Serengeti, forever in our hearts

Made in the USA
Middletown, DE
11 October 2015